空心人 1991
Empty Heart 1991

作者

黄锦婷

Author

Jinting Huang

空心人 1991

作者：黄锦婷

Empty Heart 1991

Author:

Jinting Huang

English and Chinese edition

ISBN: 9789082592092

Copyright © Jinting Huang

2018

the first print 2018

166pages

Publisher: J. Huang L G

Empty Heart 1991

Prologue in English

作品寫於 1991 年，小说中
任何比喻和意象沒有指向任
何特定的人物或事件
The work was written in
1991, any metaphor and
imagery did not point to any
particular person or event.
Empty Heart is a beautiful
heartbroken love tragedy .
In 1990, due to the war
between tribes in a tropical
region, many children lost
their families. The
International Help
Organization established a
rescue school in a safe area.
From the future, Shan met
her old truth love and the
present self. At the school,
she made a good friend
with Blanje, which is herself
in this times of the life, she
met her love future lover
Kay as well.
Ying Ying is an orphan, she
is an artistically talented
student, but the teenage

pregnancy has caused a storm in the school. Shan has helped her to survive the physical and psychological crisis, and she has offered a sex education program to a conservative school. He also helped the elderly mother Blanje to give birth to a cute little baby. Shan was struggling in the reincarnation between sadness and happiness, the attachment to love makes her hopeless, With the previous life of the gardenia, she try to wake up Kay to recognize their love, but the reality is disillusioned, she still has a good fantasy, she wrote a small note, put in the book "Longing for Life "which is both of them love to read , hoping to reunite with her true love again.

The title "Empty heart", "Empty" is one of the spirit of Eastern culture, representing does not depend on state of matter. The title of Empty Heart can be explained as people who are not spiritually attached to materialism.

The author Jinting Huang, Empty Heart 1991 was written in 1991. In her series of novels, the author likes to use "潸", "汕" or "舢" as the main name of character. The pronunciation in Chinese is the meaning of "善", means kindness. This writing habit is almost throughout all her works, forming her own uniqueness.

汕/Shan：the fish swims. (fishing, swim)

潸/Shan: tearfully

舢/Shan: the boat

Jinting Huang 's novel language and dialogue is short but not weak, boldly touches the topic of "life" and "death", with a melancholy girl temperament to dispel the serious topic, her novel has a melancholy character. Night, love loss, even abortion and other female topics will not be very easy, but the author's ethereal narrative tone brings a fresh atmosphere. Mood play a big role in her novel. Like her other novels, there are a lot of sighs, but she doesn't comment on reality .

This story is a science fiction love story. All characters are purely fictitious regardless of the living nor the death. The storyline is also fictitious, similarity is purely coincidental.

空心人 1991

中文版前言

凄美的爱情悲剧令人心碎。1990 年由于某热带地区发生部落之间的战争，很多孩子失去了家人，国际友好组织在一个安全区域建立起一所救助学校，汕从未来穿越回来，遇见自己的旧恋人和现世的自己，在学校她交到了好朋友布兰儿，就是现世的汕，遇见恋人计西也就是自己的未来的恋人 Kay,

汕的学生旃英是一名孤儿，富有艺术天分，但未成年怀孕在学校引起了风波，汕帮助旃英度过身体及心理危机难关，并向思想保守的学校提出开设少年性教育课程。汕也帮助高龄产妇 Blanje，诞下一个可爱的小宝贝。

汕在悲伤和幸福之间轮回，对爱情的执着令她欲罢不能，与前世的栀子花为约，Kay 觉得似曾相识而未能醒悟相认，现实是幻灭的，她依然抱着美好的幻想，她写下了一张小纸条，夹在《渴望生活》中，希望再度与她的真爱再度重逢。.

题目:《空心人》，"空"在东方文化中代表人的精神进入不依附于物质的平静状态。空心人在此题中可解释为精神上不附着物质主义的人。

作者黄锦婷小说写于1991年。在她系列小说中作者喜欢以"潸"，"汕"或"舢"为主人公命名字，发音都是"善"的意思，这种写作习惯几乎贯穿于她所有的作品，形成她个人独特的味道。

汕/Shan：汕,鱼游水貌。
（fishing，swim）

潸：眼泪涌上眼眶 tearfully

舢/shan：小船

她的短篇小说语言对话简洁，大胆触及"生""死"话题，但又以一种忧郁的女孩气质将严肃话题消解，她的小说具有一种忧郁的特质。黑夜，爱情失落，甚至流产等女性话题都不会很轻松，但作者空灵叙述语气却带来清新气息。和她其他的小说一样，有很多的叹息感慨，但她不对现实做评价。

小说是原创小说，版权所有，其他任何艺术形式应当被看作是盗版或侵权。这个故事是科幻爱情小说，所有人物角色无论活着的死亡的纯属虚构，故事情节属虚构，如有雷同纯属巧合，请勿对号入座。

Engl ish content

中文目录

Diary note:

Let me lead you to the world I know in my mind —————— inscription

 I closed the door and the window. The wind is still proud and resentful.

 I didn't dare to sleep, I was lying on bed with my clothes on, insomnia, I try to calm down my soul and listen to the silence of the night, after a long time, I woke up from the tiresome, , the weather is still so cold, I dress a black dress , standing in the breeze in the morning, the background is red brick and tile, the simple school building, busy with the children doing morning homework. After the wind and heavy rain, this new relief school began its daily life day after day

Shan／汕 Diary

1991, 3, 30

14

1. From the sea

Blanje who lived

next door

is just taken from a

faraway place.

Shan heard that

there is

a sea over there.

It was told that in

the imagination

somewhere

the people living

next to the beach

will not be willing to

leave their

hometown.

At first glance, Shan

can see that Blanje is a

competent woman.

Blanje was moving

from the beach to the land,

she was just like all

the housewives,

living year after year,

day after day,

and now she was

happy

having a small baby

inside her body.

The face of Blanje

showed a maternal glory

day by day, and

there was no such thing

as an 18-year-old

virgin. I remembered

the long faint long

walk with Jansen,

the breeze blew,

there was a subtle light

in the air, turning

around the corner,

Shan saw a

pregnant woman slowly

coming,

she kept staring at

her,

blurted out and said:

"I really admire her."

Kay said that any

normal woman

can do it and has

nothing to admire.

Shan was thinking

that after all,

Jansen is different

than Shan,

and what Shan

feels may not be

able to comprehend.

The difference may

be the result

that causes them to

attract each other

but eventually

cannot get together.

2. **Kay is a person**

who doesn't talk much

His favorite thing is

to play guitar

in the silent of night.

Kay is honest

and loves to do

things.

Everyone regards

him

as very close friend.   Shan

like the smell

of gardenia, Kay

give her a lot of

gardenia flowers. The

flowers

are very lively,

inserted in the bottle,

the fragrance of the

house,

many years have

passed, Shan still remember

that the fragrance

filled full the summer.

Many years have

passed.

At the dusk of that

day,

Shan suddenly

appeared

at the door of Blanje,

and now Shan think

that there is always

a feeling of being similarity.

If you can feel

someone at a

glance,

you will have a

feeling of being separated

from the world. This

feeling

will push you to

a very distant past.

Perhaps

the afterglow of the

sunset

shine on her back

and

creates a phantom

effect.

In short, her thin

shaped

and the messy in

the room

formed a strong

contrast,

so that Shan almost

suffocated,

and deeply

understood

what is called the

aesthetic tension,

the strange

question she cannot

understand

when she was in

the university class.

Shan think that

Blanje 's hometown may

also be the hometown of

Kay. It is often inexplicably

shocked by some subtle

looks or movements,

sometimes looking at B, like

watching herself.

You are a woman, and

Jansen is a man. Oh, it's

really a confused head.

In the night, Shan had a

strange dream. Shan

dreamed of a girl with a

scarlet big mouth in the room. Shan looked at her and she felt that the big mouth was so shocking and creepy. Another one came in, the same dress, and both talked in English.

　　After waking up, Shan thought about it. This has nothing to do with the image of Shan. Not all dreams have a source, and she fall asleep again. Someone knocked at the door, the secretary Phostery gave Shan a new summer schedule.

"Long time no see, Phostery." Shan say hello to Phostery. Shan only smiled and always wanted to let him to relax to have a conversion, but he is like how he always is: silent .

There are many things in the world that are invisible.

Phostery is very busy, busy in writing a notice, busy in writing test questions, busy in ringing the clock, repairing the water pipe, it seems that everything is

doing and seems to be
doing nothing...

Phostery is a young
man in his thirties. He can't
imagine such a young life
to bear so many trivial
things. Young people
should be happy, but they
are not happy. They can feel
from his back, that is the
way how you should feel
someone happy or not

Look at the way he
walks.

And how many
people are really happy in

this world?

How many people
really love you in this world?

How many people in
the world really care about
you?

How many people in
the world really care about
you what you feel?

3. Jansen

Shan received a

photo of Jansen,

wearing a denim

coat, showing

prayers in his eyes

in front of the

Buddha. Shan

didn' t know what

to do, she just

wrote a few

greetings, not a

poetry.

back to the

memories of that

night, they sat

together on the

grass, Shan swayed

his arm and asked

Jansen what the sea

looked like. He

can' t tell her in

words, he only said

that people who

had seen the sea
were different from
those who had
never seen the sea.
Shan was very
disappointed, and
her heart is so eager
to seek an answer.

What is inside
Jansen' s mind?
She wants to know
everything about
him!

Blanje considered
her pregnancy is not a big
deal at all, she takes it easy,

she did not even go to the
hospital to check whether
the fetal position is normal.
Blanje 's husband is not
around, which makes Blanje
more independent and do
everything by herself. Blanje
get a lot of opportunities to
exercise her living skills.
Buying rice, shopping ,
raising water and cooking ,
these trivial things, Blanje
had taken it, she didn't
think she has any feeling of
weight bearing.

     sometimes, a person
is in danger, people around

him get worry about him
and the person in danger
feeling nothing.

This is how things
happened sometimes.

4. TT and
Jansen

After dinner,
Shan and Blanje
sat idle in front
of their rooms,
talking
something.
Blanje suddenly

Mysteriously

approached

Shan and

whispered:

"I know

Sam's love

life secrets.

Blanje said,

Sam came

from a

section of

the corridor.

Sam was a

math

teacher and

lived next to

Blanje.

For Sam, the

impression

of Shan has

always been

very

indifferent.

Maybe there

is

something

called fate

between

people. You

have no

connection

with him. He

is a

someone

you know

and can't

communicate with.

This is the situation

with Shan and Sam. From

his point of view, could be

the same thought. But Shan

didn' t think Sam has time

to think about it. Sam is a

career-oriented person, so

young as Shan, but he

certainly does more than

Shan, because he wants

more things, and he wants

everything very clear. He

has a lot of plans. He plans to find a wife in 1990, a master degree in 1991, a lovely son in 1995, and the most professional professor in that field in 2022. He even thought of it. In the future, people can't avoid philosophical thinking, but he thinks that is a little scared, so he doesn't think so much.

Shan used to think that she was the most confused person in the world. She didn' t have any

special noble ideals. She
only believed that her left
foot must be taken out on
her right foot. She often
dresses casually for this, she
doesn＇t want to pack
herself, a woman doesn＇t
dress up means that she
has no contention with the
world. In order to cover up
this weakness, she often
smears lipstick on her lips
and erases it, wear it on
again and again, it seems as
if it has several layers and it
has a heavy silk feeling. If
the weather is bad, then the

red will be a bit tragic, so there will be a feeling of self-protection in the psychological. Jansen often asked her: Do you want to show so many lipsticks?

Shan once sent a telegram to Kay. The telegram wrote this: "Please forget TT, don't look for TT again." TT is Kay's nickname for Shan, just like a code name, Shan is TT. Shan call herself TT in the novel she wrote , and Jansen said that TT is not just two letters, it seems like two nails, and

her feelings are embedded

in someone, no one can

afford to.

     She was willing to just

make a joke with Kay, but

She'd never thought that

Kay has never given any

letter since then.

     How dark the night

is, walking around on a

small campus, trying to

reduce the restlessness

feeling, imagining Kay's

room by the sea, is the light

in the cabin? Is he talking

and laughing with his friend?
Or he was sitting alone in
the dark room with his
guitar, not fiddling, thinking
about TT, how suddenly she
just no more contact with
him? Who is TT? Did TT
really exist in his life?

Who is TT? Who is
Jansen? Time and space are
interlaced. It is said that
Jansen has not received the
telegram from Shan, and
perhaps even he does not
know Shan.
Jansen, do you know?

Shan's hair is long. Now
she has a beautiful black
hair like silk shawl.

5. Small bell

Shan is preparing lessons. A
little girl came in her room,
her name is Small bell, small
bell, she said she has no
toys, very stuffy, want to
play games with her. Shan
said let's do a guessing
game! She used to ask her
what she will do when she
grows up in the future. She
said she want to be a hotel
waiter. This child reminds
Shan of her unhappy
childhood. She didn't
know if all the children are
unhappy like this. She

doesn' t know that if other people could have a feeling of smile for the children who have **slipped over the mathematics class**.

What naughty kid

Shan' childhood…

Shan Wrote on a lot of small pieces of paper: little bells, mom, dad, lamb, stars, flowers

Also asked Small bell wrote verbs on a small piece of paper: eat water, buy, run, jump, go to school, go to sleep, go to the streets.

Shan wrote a bunch of

words on a small piece of

paper: happy, beautiful,

excited, beautiful, innocent,

beautifully

Small bell wrote down

all the places she

remembered: in the room,

in the toilet, in the cup, in

the quilt, in the market , in

the building , in the

classroom

Small bells put the

words of the four groups in

four small saucers, and all

the papers were smashed

into a small round, Small

bell pick out a small note.

The first phrase that Small

bell pick out was a lamb,

excited in the cup, running.

Connected together,

"The lamb runs excitedly in

the cup."

The second little note made

Small bell laugh and

laughed: "Flowers are

happy to do shopping in

the classroom"

After a while, Small

bells unfolded all the scraps

of paper and handed them

to the hands of the Shan,

moving the books in the bookcase to the desk.

She said: "Now, you may buy the books." She started the business of selling books at the other side of the desk. She played a game of doing business with Shan.

Whose child is Small bell?

Shan feel faintly that some things are happening slowly in invisible places.

6. Sam

Shan haven't seen
Phostery in these few days.
She used to see Phostery
walking from the office to
the office. Now he asked to
leave for a while and
everyone was at a loss. In
the past, when Shan took a
piece of chalk and teaching
equipment, as long as she
shouted "Phostery!",
Phostery could magically
find out what she needed
from the corner, so Shan
was not used to it in these

days, this is the same feeling of other people. If something is needed, they will blame that why Phostery is not there. They started to warry that Phostery will not back to work here. Everyone is tired of preparing for the lesson, the topic of all day long is about Phostery/舫, saying that if he applies for the administrative staff of an international clothing company, he will not come back, and some people say that Phostery may not really like to be here in the school, why should he go away? In a word, everyone's thoughts were swayed, and each of them had a boring head and went to do their own thing.

In the past few days when Phostery was left, B fill in his duty to do some things, such as ringing the bell when there was no electricity, and printing the exam papers. Blanje, as Administrative Assistant of the Principal's office, she moved from the office downstairs to the upper floor. In the same office as Director Loever of the Training Office, Director Loever has a thin bruin face and he is looks thin but strong. Director Hail' s office has an old record player. After working for a while, he will put a piece of Cantonese opera "The Cloud Chasing the Moon" and enjoy it alone. The overseas Chinese in these tropical jungles, Cantonese operas are the nostalgia

they cherish in their hearts.

Blanje was often

forgetting to ring the bell for

the break, Director Loever

often skips classes three

minutes , he walked from the

teaching building to the office

to ring the bell.

Later, I heard that

Loever was in order to sign

her wife in the Chinese

countryside to Nepal. He has

been working in this

international help project

school for many years. How

many years have been

blurred, because his wife has

50

to take care of her mother in the country, she can't be with Loever for a long time, and they are getting used to living in a long distance, but their love relationship has no problem.

7. Sam go to Europe to study

Sam received a reply from the European university's master's admission application, saying that he did make a good impression in the admissions score. If the dream came true, he would go to Europe to study in a few months. The confirmation letter was not there yet, he was exiting like an ant in the hot pot.

What a hot summer!

Jansen, this summer's sultry has make Shan feeling so upset.

"How are you doing?, I miss you so much……"she talk to Jansen by heart. This evening, the discipline meeting. Loever said that teachers should be taught by teachers. But there are also some lax management, not the atmosphere of the Do Your Best. Shan was think about Small bell, the children now and then are not really a big favor to the story of the cowherd, it was slowly

changing that they were not

having a big fun to play a role

game in their childhood.

Their consciousness, the

small seedlings of the

commercial economy began

to sprout.

8. Shan's memories

1991.6.15

It is rather to be free in

spiritual then to be pessimistic.

I was frustrated too.

I was complain a lot

In front of the hard life

53

Should take it easy like the master

of Dao in the deep mountain

How to cure your own pain:

1, do not demand too much for

yourself

2, to see your own experience

with an open mind, but only a

drop in the ocean

3, observe life

4, pay attention to people

Many years ago, Jansen looked at her eyes and said, "TT, do not be hang around everywhere anymore, okay?" Jansen is afraid to be moving to another place. Once she is very happy to be alone, like a bird spreads her wings, Jansen cannot accept it.

"Hey, are you going to settle down? Stuck in one place, no longer moving. "Jansen said,   "I will not move."

Shan was feeling so sad for the conversation.

If Shan continue her current work and continue to be happy by her own life, and Jansen is no longer wandering, no longer moving, then the world is so big that

they will not have the day of
reunion.

tonight, Shan didn't
sleep very well, and the girl
with a scarlet mouth was
disturbing in her dream.

9. the office

In the big office, the
atmosphere was abnormal.
They are in groups of three
and five, whispering. When
they saw Shan coming in,
they suddenly fell silent. Sam
just sitting on his chair, a
cigarette in his mouth. "An
old virgin gave lesson to a
disciple who has an
illegitimate daughter." He

said that while he was turning

in the wicker chair, and Shan

saw that Blanje was not

responding on what

happened.

Shan was shocked.

Walked out of the office

Blanje chased him

up and said, "TT, the student

who learned painting with

you is in trouble."

"What happened?"

Shan asked.

"She is pregnant."

"How is it possible,

the girl who is pure as jade?"

"TT, Sam talked bad

things about you, what are

you going to do?"

"He is right,

Ying Ying is really in trouble."

"I still remember that I also know his secrets, her girlfriend... Why don't you set a fire in the topic, so that he can't get the stairs?"

"Oh, forget it, Sky is a net, that is way of saying, let it be how it should be, things about his girlfriend is not my concerned, he has his own reason, well the "old aunt" is an awkward name, but, well...... I also have my own way to live on. "

58

"Your way is very good, but there is a kind of well-known truth in this society, that is morality. He should not attack on you like this way."

"Hey, don't be stuck on this things , we are not the kind of people who like to win in the final words, we are not like those women who only talked the whole day."

"But TT, I feel weird. Some people evade moral constraints and live leisurely the entire life; some people's life is to put on the shoes of morality, but you don't seem to be both."

I only have a bitter smile.

Shan is a person who is rich in rhythm in the inner world and does not put this change into action, so Shan is just Shan.

It's hard to tell the story.

Perhaps only Jansen can use the sixth feeling to perceive what kind of person she is, because Jansen and Shan are not labeling people and things.

Jansen always said that the future is unknowable, and there are many people and things waiting for us, right? TT?

"Director Loever, I hope that the school leaders

will consider it again. Can you change the mind of Ying Ying, just let her stay in school?"

Loever's face is more and more worry: "There is no way to change it. Your student's trouble is big enough. I heard that you also taught her to paint the body image without clothes. Is there such a thing?"

"That is an angel portrait..." He still tried to defend. "The foundation of the nude studio, without the knowledge of the structure of the human body, it is impossible to draw a well-dressed or covered up body. Director Loever, Ying ying has a certain talent in painting..."

"TT, do you know how the teachers talk about you behind?"

"The mouth is long on others, but you can't control it." "What Ying Ying need right now is care, not punishment ..."

Get out of the office. The only good elder person in the school are against it, knowing that things have been difficult to recover.

On a very warm night, the campus was asleep. He

walked around on campus.

Lights of the room of Phostery are on.

Shan Knocking on the door.

"I know it is you, TT." He said, "You are the only one who has the problem of night walking in this school."

"It's not fair to blame anyone, you don't have a good sleep." Shan sighed.

"Don't blame everyone, I know that you are sad for Ying Ying." He try to comfort her "Don't be sad, TT, once people think about what responsibility they have to bear, there is no way to love."

"Sometimes, responsibility is much more useful than love." Shan said.

"TT, if you have ever been in love, you will not say that, it is a feeling of desperation. Ying Ying is in love, not anybody's fault."

"So, have you been in love?"

" falling in love! Yes! Not only that! I lost it and I still in love! This is the reason for my nickname of Shang, the witty voice of Hurt in Chinse culture."

It seems that the word "love" in this world is indeed ubiquitous.

64

Phostery gave a cup of tea,
and she still remembers the
coolness, sweetness and
comfort of the cup of tea.

10. the recover

In the depths of the
white corridor, Ying ying
heard the sound of metal
collision in the dark place.

It seems that after a
century, wearing a dark and
colorful dress, trying to dress
up like a young woman, Ying
ying walked out stumbled,
the makeup powder on her
face turned grey, and the eye
shadow on the upper part of
the eye was outstanding.

Surprised that the eyes did not have the fear that she should have at that age, but the vicissitudes behind the disaster.

The fate of a young girl changes in an instant. The hospital's white corridor looks lonely.

Shan want to look out the window, the sunshine outside is dazzling. Shan seems to hear the helpless voice of Ying Ying: "I shouldn't lost this child, and I should not have hesitate to spare him, I should do everything for him." She blame herself.

"Ying Ying" Shan touch her long hair, said from her heart, "You are not enough to be responsible for another life. It is a small baby, only love is not enough. You must know that the reason of love is not enough for a small life to grow up healthily. Have you said that you are eager to grow up healthily?"

"Teacher, I know that you are try to make me feel good. I still feel very sad, very sad..." Ying ying was still crying.

Shan try to make her calm down, life is a long process, rather admiring fish in the water, then it is better to retreat to the net, take a step back and think, it is much safer than swaying, but these words seems like very hard at this moment, for the injured person, can only tell her "look forward, all the sadness will pass. "Let her know that someone behind her supports her and survives the saddest moment. The most important thing is the recovery of the body, and then the psychological recovery.

      I regret that I had too little communication with the students before. However, these thoughts are just a matter of thinking. I thought that I would like to propose to the director Loever that the school should ask the teachers to set up the adolescent sexual health lectures.

The reality is that, for so many years, what do you get for your personal feelings? Regarding Kay, there is still no news. This is no longer a little game about love and a joke.

Ying Ying ate the chicken soup that she had make for her, and the soup was showed an attractive luster.

Ying Ying said: "I seems to have recovered again."

"Of course, after all, young people."

11. Baby born

"Actually, your skin is still very beautiful " Blanje's eyes praised Shan without any disguise. "This is the result of not using cosmetics."

Shan told her proudly.

Blanje is getting harder and harder to walk. Blanje suddenly had a fever after dinner, and Shan heard a faint cry from the next door.

This crying makes her feel as if the baby is restless inside the mother.

Shan stood in the room of Blanje and she don't know what to do, "go to the hospital," Blanje said helplessly with tears.

Shan dare to say that She was very scared. Because Blanje said that her expecting period will be half a month, and she is afraid that the restless little life will come to the world earlier.

"I am going to call the car!"

"Go!" Blanje almost

shouted desperately.

Blanje entered the delivery

room, a doctor's face was

pale, and he ran out calmly:

"Is the patient's husband

coming?"

My heart suddenly beating

fast.

"What happened?"

"Maternal lady are

over 40 years old, and she

was not strong, she is in an

instable situation, and the

surgery needs to be signed."

The doctor said.

"Her husband can't come

here within two days. I am

her close friend. Can I sign
it?" Shan said:
Doctor: "It can only be like
this way"
Shan Sign the name of the
Shan on the column of the
relatives of the patient. "TT."

She sat down on the
bench in the hospital corridor,
and the sky was dark outside.
After a while, the rain was
loud. Blanje 's husband may

arrive tomorrow, Shan is
concealed.

No time is so
momentary, that Shan
missed Jansen so much,
Shan remembered the dusk

that day, the slanting rain, the

autumn clothes, and the

empty dormitory from the

weekend. The heart is full of

lost, the rain boots are filled

with water, and the road is so

heavy that they can't lift their

feet. Then a wet figure

suddenly appears in front of

the eyes. Look up little by

little, that pair of cold stars in

a flash of lightning, words is

too much, that is the second

day they met in the rain,

Jansen was wet by the rain

and the image of him

became an ellipsis that could

never be forgotten in life.

Some days ago, Ying Ying

finished the chicken soup
that Shan had made for her.
Then she asked: "Teacher,
what do you want to do most
in your life?"

Walking out of the
weekend empty dormitory,
my heart is full of lost, rain
boots filled with water, and
walked up to sink the foot,
then a wet figure suddenly
appeared in front of me,
looking up little by little, the
pair of cold stars in a flash of
lightning, there is no any
word could describe the
moment of emotion.

She was woke up from the flash back by the voice of Ying Ying: "Teacher, what do you want to do most in your life?"

Shan really want to say: "I want to only love a man." But she just said to Ying Ying: "Me as your teacher, has no special ideals, I am just like everyone else."

Shan already know that it is very important to love a man. It is also important to learn not to love after love. There is no need for Ying Ying to know this so deep so far. For her, love is her only way out.

Blanje has long been classifying people like this in a group of people who don't know what it is, and the weak point of Shan does not prevent her from getting close to Blanje. The only

reason might be Blanje is

from the sea, and Blanje is

looming a little bit the figure of Jansen. At the moment when Blanje is in trouble,

only one person is by her side, which makes Shan think of her husband. Shan can't imagine the appearance of Blanje' husband should be.

His appearance does not matter with Shan, but this time he should be coming.

12. reunion

Shan saw a tall man moving towards this side, the brownish skin covered all the darkness, his footsteps rushed, and the upper body leaned forward slightly, which reminded me of the eagerly looking for Shan on the platform of station. The embarrassing Jansen, the train is about to start, but he is still so anxious, the upper body was slight tilt , searching for Shan, which

gives a very childish

impression, and Shan even

get a maternal feeling: a man

sometimes is also vulnerable

like a child.

Shan was calm at that

moment, and in her girl times

she thinks that she is the kind

of woman with strong

mentality. The world is

always warmer and softer

because she is a woman.

She didn't let him kiss his

forehead, but he repeatedly

tied the scarf again and again:

Dear, you should be careful

on the road, take care! Shan

wearing a black dress,

carrying a heavy travel bag, standing next to the messy running tour, the young man at the consignment smiled and smiled.

"TT, don't you go around, waiting for me, okay?"

"What about you? Are you waiting for me?"

"Oh, I wait for you."

The voice of dialogue many years ago is still in Shan's ear.

"Jansen----------."

Shan almost screamed, the corridor in the hospital was awakened by her scream, many mysterious closed doors suddenly revealed a suspicious gap, from the door slits with a piece of unkempt.

"Jansen, you are coming!" Shan shook his arm sadly, and the tears broke out like a dam.
"I don't know who is Jansen ." Jansen said. At the end of the corridor, a white car slowly parked over, and Shan saw that the most familiar thing with her was that the eyes that had appeared in the depths of memory many times eagerly looked over there.

Jansen bent down

his body and face to Blanje,

talk to her softly, Blanje 's

pale face was spoiled, she
was happy, even though she
had just returned from the
death line, she had a child in
her middle-aged and she had
the happiness.

In the nightmare Shan
sees a lot of letters on the
body, making her feel
suffocated.
In my sleep Shan fell into the
boundless abyss, and many
familiar faces rushed to the
dream realm...
If you have no distractions

and no concerns, you can enjoy happiness and elegance in the world. She knows in my heart that she was going to break free, and she wanted to have fun in this world. If she wanted to reincarnate, she will meet Jansen again, and she will not become a grass. She was thinking the face of Jansen, he appears, his eyes are mournful. Looking at Shan that went with the wind, he seemed to be incomparably in a hurry. He reached out and grabbed her hand... He saved Shan.

When Shan woke up,
Ying ying was eating biscuits
in the room.

"Teacher, I am coming
back."

"Is it?" Shan felled her
heart is old.

13. Ying Ying returned to school

Ying Ying's return to
school, her work was
attributed to the exhibition
which she participated last
year, and her painting "Girls"
which participated in the
exhibition saved her. It was a
nude oil painting work with
her own model. If Director

84

Loever knows that this painting won the prize, he will be whispering to himself: the world is not the oldest. The School of Art, specially wanted Ying Ying to be in their Art school, can be exempted from direct professional painting, and the school recruits Ying Ying. "Teacher, you have to learn flowers with you." Ying Ying said.

After dinner, riding a bicycle, Shan got outside the city alone. Whenever there was something unsatisfactory, she could only go to the suburbs and give himself to nature.

This place has never been seen. There are some grasses on the low ridges. A group of tombs stand there. Unknown small rosy flowers are open in the tomb.

The deceased has been gone with the earth.

They must not feel lonely. But their lives have been loved. The psychology of Shan is gradually filled with sorrow. What is life, come with hope, or leave with dissatisfaction. People, the thirst for love is never limited.

Shan don't know why,
so much sentimentality, as if
a love story tells her
something, this story is far
from the city, and it's gentle
and honest, and the sky is
full of this story.

She knew that she had not
explained all the meanings of
life, but she knew that she 'd
given her love to Jansen, the
man who both self-
confidence and wisdom.

Everything is doomed.
What can be changed?

14. The Gardenia flower

The sunset of the sunset is
still burning, and the tired
birds are quietly
inhabiting their respective
trees. On the other side of
the forest, there is a white
cloud, like a dazzling
mountain.

At the foot of the
mountain, Shan picked a
baby flower of gardenia with ,
and inserted it into the vase
of the desk.

The figure of a
person enters the feeling of
Shan. He stood at the door
and suddenly turned back,
imagining his eyes looking at

him with deep affection,
imagining that she was so
affectionately calling him
"Jansen", and she only
looked at him silently.
She thought in her heart, this
is Jansen, although
sometime he is faraway, she
can always feel about him.

He looked at the
gardenia on the table and
said, "Why, those residual
flowers, have you not
removed?"

He looked at the
book, "Longing for Life" and
said, "Why are you still
reading this book?" He
signed his your handwriting

89

on the title page of this book:
"Maybe you will fail many
times, and eventually you
can express yourself, and
that performance will prove
your life."

"Over these years, I
have only lived for this
sentence." Shan told Jansen.

Jansen said: "TT, you
have grown up."

Jansen touched the
hair of Shan and found the
vicissitudes of the forehead.

"TT," his hoarse voice
whispered, and he printed his
lips on his forehead.

"TT, you really
deserve to be loved," he said.

"Can I come in?"

There was a polite voice behind Shan, interrupting the meditation of Shan.

"Of course ."

"TT, thank you for taking care of Blanje "

He took the gardenia on the table and said that it was really fragrant.

He also pointed to "Long for Life" and said, "Are you longing to life"?

"Are you surprised?" she asked.

Jansen: "I thought that only one person likes this book."

"Blanje doesn't like it?" she tempted him.

"No, she is a pure family woman who never cares about art."

He said, "So what seems to be a woman who is not too pure?"

"Maybe, you are a little deferent then other women ." He was embarrassed.

"It doesn't matter, I would rather be ugly than to be hypocritical."

"You are very interesting." His eyes suddenly filled with vitality, and this is familiar for Shan.

"Thank you for your highest remark." Shan know that Jansen's highest comment on women is "very interesting." He has stood up and ready to leave, and his body stopped suddenly, and the twilight really came.

People can't step into a river at the same time. This is what philosophers have already said. The past is gone, just like the countless pieces of waste paper that have been torn off on the calendar. These days will always be more or less life. A little trace of the annual ring, or beautiful or ugly.

In fact, what surprised Shan was that, like a spirit, it was turning back the clock. This is the same time that she entered the river with the Jansen. But this time is of course different. Her feeling is that she has arranged the plot to move towards the original river step by step.

Ying Ying has not come to me for a long time. Except Blanje, Phostery and Ying Ying, Shan has not made other friends in this school. She believes that she is equally important to them. If one day they left me and I can't find them anymore,

what kind of life will it be?

She had read the Buddha's

book these days, and she

always like to think about the

fate, the fate and so on.

15. Loever

The weather in the

south of June was very hot.

She just went to the hospital

to visit Director Loever.

Director Loever suddenly

fainted in hospital this

morning, his blood sugar was

too low.

Under the school bus

stop sign, Ying Ying carries a

picture clip, and her long hair

is bundled into a hand, and a
loose white T-shirt reflects
the darkness of her face.
After all, youth is youth. No
matter which angle you
appreciate, it will always be
beautiful.
"Ying ying, the sun is
burning……such hot whether
are you going to paint
outside?"

"Go to the Botanical
Garden, where the city's
coolest place."
Ying Ying stopped talking,
the bus came, her yellow hair
flashed and disappeared.

Shan was left behind
under the stop sign, alone.

She really admires the ease of Ying Ying. She can't think of the 30-year-old look of Ying ying. What else can she have in addition to being relaxed and beautiful? A woman has beauty and vitality, and that is a very successful woman.

Last night, Loever also told him: "TT, I understand that young people are more emotional, who is not being youth?

I want to remind you as an elder, you should stay out of things.

I know that bad things are passed down for

thousands of miles, but what makes you sadder is that Loever has gave her a completely pertinent attitude, making it difficult to distinguish. Sam was on the side, engraved with wax paper that he could never finish. The tip of the pen gave a uniform, indifferent voice.

She has read a notes today: "life is more important than business" Everyone knows that life is short, but since people think life is important as business , the world can't enjoy the fun of Taishang Laojun's alchemy. From this point, modern

People are really not as smart as the ancients.

He smelled the scent of gardenia.

16. again the smell of gardenia 98

"It's too early to pick up, the flower bones haven't opened yet, and it will fade after waiting for it to open up." Shan told Kay, the plot was exactly the same as it was a few years ago. The tidal tide slowly drowned me.

"This is the last gardenia in the summer, and it is hard to find." Shan said. Her tears flowed silently. The

weather was so hot, she got
up and picked up a wet towel,
she cleaned up the tears on
her face.

"The wind is not the
end, the rain is not the end of
the day, familiar with this?
Heaven and earth. Heaven
and earth cannot be long;
how could people change it?"
Dao Classical scripture said
so.

Separation is

inevitable,

But at the

same time it

is destined to

get together.

Always

drifting deep

inside

Like the

separation of

the sea and

the land

Just like

spring and

winter

Can't

Meet

 each other

However one

day

You will be at

the corner of

the street

appear again.

Appear again

In my dreams

In front of my

eyes..

we will be

together

1991.6.9

once you are in the

world

as one day in the

heaven sky

Eternally

Longing for a lot of

love!

Desire to be

hugged by you,

close your eyes

safely, wait for your

kiss

Desire to display a

lot of love

This moment you

appreciate in a

small corner

Longing for tears

toughing my heart

Oh, it seems that

the days are not

going to get to the

head.

miss you...

----from 氵山 diary

Kay is
leaving, and
Shan put this
note in the
book
"Longing for
Life" and
gave it to Kay.
Kay's car
disappeared

104

at the end of

the path..

空心人 中文版

作品寫於 1991 年，任何比喻和意象沒有指向任何特定的人物或事件

The work was written in 1991, any metaphor and imagery did not point to any particular person or event.

引：让我引领着你，走向我所想象中认知的世界------题记

关上门，关上了窗，风依然骄傲幽怨。

这样的夜，我不敢熟睡，合衣躺在床上，失眠，屏神谛听着夜的寂静，过了很久，累了，醒来，天气依然是那么地冷，我是一个黑衣黑裙的少女，站在清晨的微风中，背景是红砖碧瓦，简陋的校舍，忙着做早

106

功课的孩子。大风大雨过后，

这个新生的救济学校，开始它

每天日复一日的生活......汕日

记 1991 · 3 · 30

1，从海边来

隔壁的布兰儿，

是刚刚从很远的地方牵来，听说那地方有海，既然有海，为什么舍得离开，在汕的想象中，海边的人是不会舍得离开自己的故乡的。

汕一眼便看得出来布兰儿是一个称职的女人，布兰儿从海边迁到陆地，如陆地上所有的家庭主妇一般年复一年，日复一日地生活，她的肚子里怀着一个小生命，布兰儿的脸上一日比一日显出一种母性的光彩，是十八岁的处子也没有的。汕想起很久很久以前与计

西散步的那个黄昏，微风习习，
空中有一种微妙的光线在流动，
转过街角，看见一个孕妇慢慢
地走来，汕一直盯视着她看，
脱口而出说："我真佩服她。"

Kay 说任何正常的妇
女都能做得到，有什么好佩服
的。

汕心想毕竟计西与汕
不同，汕感受到的东西 KAY
未必能领会，不同也许是导致
汕们互相吸引但最终走不到一
起的结局。

2. Kay 是一个不太爱说话的人

Kay 是一个不太爱说话的人，他最喜欢的事是在夜深人静时谈谈吉他，KAY 老实，又爱做事，大家都把他当成自己的朋友。

汕很喜欢栀子花的味道，KAY 就冒着被罚的危险，给汕摘来许许多多的栀子花。花开很盛，插在瓶子里，满屋的香，很多年过去了，汕还记得，那香味弥漫了一个夏天。

很多年就过去了。

那天的黄昏汕突然出现在布兰儿的门口，现在回想起来老有一种恍如隔世的感觉。
如果汕一眼便能感觉到某个人，
汕就会有隔世的感觉，这种感
觉将汕推至非常遥远的过去，
也许是夕阳的余晖打在她的背
上造成幻影的效果，总之，她
的瘦骨形销与汕房间的杂乱形
成强烈的对比，使汕差点窒息，
汕深深理解了什么叫做美学上
的张力，那个大学课堂上怎么
也弄不明白的古怪问题。

汕觉得布兰儿的故乡
说不定也是 Kay 的故乡，汕
常常莫名奇妙地被某些微妙的
神情或动作所震撼，有时看着
布兰儿，像看着自己。

汕是女人，计西是男人。汕真是脑袋糊涂。

夜里做了一个奇怪的梦，梦见汕的房间里走进来一位涂着猩红大嘴巴的女孩，汕打量着她，只觉得那个大嘴巴那么触目惊心，令人毛骨悚然。又进来一位，一样的打扮，两位都操着英语与汕交谈。

醒来后想了想，这与汕的形象绝对无关，并不是所有的梦都有源头，汕复又沉沉入睡。

有人敲门，干事觥给汕送来新的夏令作息表。

"好久不见了，觞。"

汕打招呼。觞只笑了笑，总是想引他多说一句，但他这人就是这样。

这世界上有许多汕看不清的东西。

觞很忙，忙着写通知，忙着刻印测验试题，忙着敲钟，修水管，似乎什么都干又似乎无所事事......

觞是一个三十多岁的年轻人，想象不出如此年轻的生命要承担这么多琐事，年轻人是应该快乐一些，可是觞不快乐，从他的背影就能够感觉

得到，一个人快步快乐，看他
走路的样子就知道了。

而这世上真正快乐的
人有几人？

这世上真正爱你的有
几个人？

这世界上真正在乎你
的有几个人？

这世界上真正关心你
的有几个人？

3. 计西

收到计西的照片，穿
着牛仔衣，做在佛前，双眼流
露着祈祷，不知怎么汕就随手

写下那几个问好。不算是诗歌吧。

那一夜他们一起坐在草地上，汕向他打听大海是什么样子，汕摇晃着他的胳膊求他告诉汕，他只说见过大海的人和没见过大海的人是不一样的。

汕很失望，汕寻求答案的心是如此急切。

计西这个人啊！

布兰儿也算身怀六甲了，可她并不着急，她甚至没上过医院检查一下胎位是否正常。布兰儿的丈夫不在身边，这就使得布兰儿什么都是身体力行。使得布兰儿得到不少锻炼的机会。买米买菜，提水烧饭，这些琐碎的事，布兰儿都承担了，并不觉得她有什么负重的感觉。

很多时候，一个人身临险境，他自己不觉而局外的人看了不禁替他汗颜。

世上很多事都是如此。

4. TT 和计西

晚饭后，汕与布兰儿闲闲地坐在各自的房门前，天南地北地闲聊。布兰儿突然神秘地凑近小声地说：""汕知道 Sam 的感情秘密。"布兰儿说着，Sam 从走廊的一段走过来，Sam 是一位数学老师，住在布兰儿的隔壁。

对于 Sam，汕的印象一直很淡漠。也许人和人之间有一种叫缘分的东西。你与他没有缘分，他就是与你做了一世邻居，也无法与你沟通。

汕与 Sam 就是这样的情况，从他的角度来看，也未尝不是这样。但汕想 Sam 是没有时间去瞎想这些的，Sam 是一个事业型的人，与汕一样的年轻，但理所当然地比汕更有所作为，因为他想要的东西

比汕多，而且他想要的每一样
东西都很明确，他的计划很多，
计划 90 年找一个老婆，91 年
读硕士，

95 年生个大胖儿子，
2022 年做那个领域最专业的
教授，他甚至很想到将来的，
人不可回避的哲学思考，但他
想了有些害怕，所以他就不去
想那么多了。

汕曾以为自己是世上
最糊涂的人，汕没有什么特别
高尚的理想，只相信左脚迈出
后

必定是右脚迈出，为

这个汕经常衣着随便，从不好

好

收拾自己。女人不打

扮。意味着她与世无争，为了

掩盖这一弱点，汕经常随便地

在嘴唇上

涂抹上口红。抹掉。

再图上。仿佛上了几层。有重

磅真丝的感觉。

倘若天气坏。那红就

显得有些悲壮，这样就会在心

理上有一种自我

保护的感觉。计西以

前就经常问汕：你不要图这么

多口红好吗？

汕曾经给 Kay 打过一次电报，电报是这样写的：

"请忘记 TT 吧，

不要再找 TT。" TT 是 Kay 对汕的昵称，就像一种代号，汕就是 TT.

汕喜欢在小说中将自己称为 TT, 而计西说 TT 不仅仅是两个字母，它好像两颗钉子，她的感情嵌到谁身上，谁也拨不掉。

汕愿意只是和 Kay 开个玩笑，竟想不到 Kay 从此以后一直未给汕片言只语。

夜是多么的黑，汕在
不大的校园里走来走去，试图
消除汕内心的

躁动不安，汕想象着
海边 Kay 的小屋，小屋里亮
着灯吗？他在与他的朋友门谈
笑吗？或者他独自坐在黑黑的
屋里怀抱着吉他，也不拨弄，

呆呆地想着 TT,怎么就
突然从他的生活消失了呢？TT
是谁？TT 难道真的曾经存在
于他的生活中吗？

TT 是谁？计西又是谁？
时空交错。这么说计西还没有
收到汕的电报，或许甚至他根
本不认识汕。

计西，知道吗？汕的
头发又长了。现在汕拥有一头
美丽的黑缎子一样的披肩发。

5. 小铃铛

汕正在备课。跑进来
小铃铛，小铃铛，她说她没有
玩具，很闷，想和她做游戏。

汕说那

汕们做猜谜游戏？汕
习惯地问她将来长大要做什么？
她说她做饭店服务员。这小孩
让汕想起自己的不快乐的童年，

不知是不是所有的小孩

都像这样不快乐，也
不知所有的大人都像汕一样，
对跷课的孩子都有一种会心一

笑的感觉，曾经的调皮的

汕......

汕在很多小纸片上写

下：小铃铛 妈妈 爸爸 小羊 星

星 花儿

又叫小铃铛在小纸片

上写下动词：

吃 水 买 奔跑 跳 去 上

学 睡觉 上街

汕又在小纸片上写上

一堆词语：高兴地 美丽 地 激

动地 漂亮地 天真地 好看地

小铃铛把所有她想起

来的地点写下来：

在房间 在厕所 在杯
子 在被子在市场 在楼房 在教
室

汕叫小铃铛把这四个
小组的词语放在四个小茶碟中，
所有纸条揉成一小团，叫小铃
铛从中

抽出一个小纸条。

结果小铃铛抽出的第
一个词组是小羊，在杯子里，
激动地，奔跑

连起来就是"小羊在
杯子里激动地奔跑"

第二个小纸条令小铃
铛哈哈大笑："花儿在教室里
高兴地上街"

过了一会，下铃铛又把所有的碎纸片展开，递到汕的手中，把书柜里的书搬到书桌上.

她说："现在，你们来买书。"她在书桌子的另一端做起了卖书的生意。汕和她玩起了做生意的游戏。

小铃铛究竟是谁家的孩子？

汕隐隐地觉得，一些事情正在汕看不见得地方慢慢地发生。

6. 觞

这几日不见了觞的影子，看惯了觞从这个办公室晃到那个办公室，这下他请假走了，一下子大家都不知所措。

以往领个粉笔，教学用具什么的，只要大叫一声"觞"，觞就会不知从那个角落里拿出所需要的东西，所以这几天

大家都不习惯，少了什么东西，就埋怨觞怎么不回来，大家备课累了，在一起的话题就是觞，说觞这次若应聘考上一个国际服装公司的行政

人员，他就不回来了，又有人
说觞或许是真的

不喜欢这所学校，他
为什么要走呢？一句话沟起了
大家的心事，各自有闷着头，
干自己的事去了。

觞请假的这几天，布
兰儿就代替他做一些事，比如
没电的时候

打打下课铃，印考试
试卷什么的，布兰儿因做训导
处的干事，她每天从楼下的办
公室搬到楼上，与训导处的
Loever 同一间办公室，
Loever 一张瘦黄的脸，一副
老黄牛的样子。

Loever 的办公室有一部老唱机，工作了一会，他会放上一段粤曲《彩云追月》，独自品味。他们这些热带丛林里的华侨，粤曲是他们珍藏于内心的乡愁。

布兰儿的记性很差，经常忘了打铃，Loever 就经常提前三分钟下课，

从教学楼里小跑到办公室敲钟。

后来听布兰儿说，Loever 是为了把她在中国乡下的老婆签到尼泊尔，他在这件国际援助学校

干了很多年，究竟多少年都已经模糊了，因为老婆在乡下

有老母需要照顾，她一直无法长期地和 Loever 在一起，

他们也渐渐习惯了远距离的分居生活，但他们感情是没有问题的。

7，Sam 要去欧洲读书

Sam 接到了欧洲大学硕士入学申请回复，

说他在录取排名中成绩优秀，信中要他等待最后的确认答复。这么说如果梦想成真，

再过几个月，他就要去欧洲读书了。但是确定函迟迟未来，Sam 如热锅上的蚂蚁。

今年的夏天真热啊。

计西，这个夏天的闷热使汕所坚持的原则土崩瓦解。

计西啊，你过得好不好呢？

今天晚上，训导处开会。Loever 讲话，说老师应该为人师表，

有上进心，学无止境，专研教学。但也有些松懈了自汕管理，没有上进心的风气。

百无聊赖之际汕不禁想起在汕的房间摆书摊的小铃铛，

现在的小孩，他们不要听牛郎织女的故事，他们更不会玩过家家的游戏，他们的意识里，商业经济的小幼苗开始萌芽。

*

8.汕的回忆

1991.6.15

与其悲观，不如旷达
对待人生，也曾失意，也曾抱
怨，在生活的重压下，拿出仙
风道骨的潇洒。

怎么对待自己的痛苦：

1， 对自己不要要求
过高

2， 用开放的心态去
看自己的经历，
只不过沧海一粟

3， 观察生活

4， 注重人

------汕日记自勉

131

很多年前，计西看着汕的眼睛说："TT，不要再逍遥了，好吗？"计西害怕汕逍遥，一旦真的逍遥，如鲲鹏一般展翅而去，计西施接受不了这个事实的。

汕说，那你呢，你要安定下来吗？固定地在一个地方，不再搬家。计西说："我不会搬家了。"

汕心悲伤。

如果汕继续目前的工作，继续逍遥，而计西不再流浪，不再搬家，那么天地之大，汕们不会有相逢重聚的那一天了。

这一夜，睡得不甚安宁，那个猩红大嘴的女孩又来扰汕平静。

9. 办公室

大办公室，气氛异常。他们三五成群，切切私语。看到汕进来，顿时鸦雀无声。Sam 刚好背着汕坐着，他嘴里一根香烟，"一个老处女带着一个有私生女的门徒。"说着他身子在藤椅中转动了一圈，汕同事看到布兰儿没有反应的侧影。

汕心一惊。转身退出办公室。

汕追上来对汕说："TT，跟你学画画的学生旖英遇到麻烦了。"

"什么事？"汕问。

"她怀孕了。"

"怎么可能，那个纯洁如玉的女孩？"

"TT，Sam 这样说你坏话，你打算怎么办啊？"

"他说得都对啊，旖英确实遇到了麻烦。"

"还记得汕说过汕也知道他的秘密吗，她女朋友……你何不也放他一把火，让他也下不了台阶？"

"汕，算了，天网恢恢，疏而不漏，该怎么样就怎么样，他女友怎么样不关我的事，他有他的道理，我当我的老姑婆。我也有我自己的道理。"

"你的道理很好，但这个社会还有一种人们公认的道理，那就是道德。他这样攻击你不应该。"

"汕，你也这么傻，汕们都不是那种喜欢在嘴巴上赢的人，我们不是喜欢清谈的女人。"

"可是 TT，汕觉得奇怪呀，有的人一生规避道德的约束，活得悠哉游哉；有的人一生的目的就在于套上道德这双鞋子，可你呢，似乎两者都不是。"

汕只有苦笑。

汕是属于哪种内心世界富于律动而没有把这种变化付诸行动的人，于是汕就什么都不是了。

妙处难与君说。

也许只有计西能用第六感觉感知到汕是怎么样一个人，因为计西和汕一样，对人对事从不贴上标签。

计西总是说未来是不可知的，还有许多的人和事等着汕们，对吗？TT？

"Loever，汕希望学校领导再考虑一下，能不能把勒令退学改为留校察看？"

Loever 焦黄的脸愈加焦黄："没有办法呀。"你的学生痛的漏子够大了，听说你还叫教她画脱光了衣服的人体像，有没有这回事？"

"那是天使画像……"汕仍然努力辩解。"裸体画室基础，没有人体结构形态知识，不可能画好衣着的或被遮掩的人体。Loever，旆英在画画方面有一定的天赋……"

"TT，你知道背后老师们怎么议论你妈？"

"嘴长在别人身上，汕管不着。"汕吼道。"旆英

136

现在需要的是关心而不是打击……"

走出闷热异常的训导处。学校唯一的老好人都反对汕，汕知道事情已经很难挽回了。

很热的晚上，校园沉睡了。汕在校园里走来走去。

觞的灯亮着。

汕敲门。

"汕知道是你，TT."觞说，"全校老师只有你有夜游的毛病。"

"怪老天爷不公平，汕没有好的睡眠。"汕直叹气。

"别这么怨天尤人，汕知道你为旖英的事情难过。"觞安慰汕道，"别难过了，TT，人一旦想到要承担什么责任，那就没有办法去爱了。"

137

"可有时候，责任比爱
要有用得多。"汕说。

"TT，你要是恋爱过，
就不会这么说，那是一种不顾
一切的感情。旖英陷入了恋爱，
不是谁的过错。"

"这么说，你恋爱
过？"

"岂止恋爱，我还失恋
过呢。这就是我的名字觞的来
由，觞谐音伤。"

看来，这人世间的
"情"字，确实是无处不在的。

觞给汕斟了一杯茶，
汕至今仍能忆起那杯茶的清凉、
甘甜和安慰。

10. 康复

挺过这最难过的时刻

旖英在白色走廊的深
处，光线幽暗的地方传来金属
碰撞的声音。

似乎是过了一个世纪，
穿着深色斑斓衣服，竭力把自
己打扮得像个少妇的旖英跌跌
撞撞地走了出来，脸上的化妆
粉变成灰白的一片，眼睛上部
的眼影格外地突出，汕惊异于
那双眼睛没有她那个年龄应该
有的恐惧，而是大劫之后的沧
桑。

一个少女的命运转变
在顷刻之间。医院白色的长廊
显得寂寞。

汕想窗外看去，外面
的阳光多耀眼啊。汕似乎听到
旖英无助的声音："汕要这个

孩子，为他受苦受累汕也在所
不惜。"

"旖英啊，"汕抚摸
着她软而长的头发，耐着心说"
你现在还不能足以对另一个生
命负责，降生下来就是一个小
生命，而不是谁的宠物或玩具，
仅仅有爱，远远不够，你须知
道爱情的理由还不能足够一个
小生命健康地长大成人，你不
是说过你渴望健康地长大吗？
"

"老师，汕知道你在
安慰汕，汕还是感到很伤心，
很伤心……"旖英还在哭泣。

汕想安慰她，生命是
一个漫长的过程，以其羡慕鱼
儿在水中逍遥自在，不如退而
结网，做什么事情，退后一步
想，比摇摇晃晃前进来得稳妥
得多，但这些话再此刻显得多

么生硬，对于受伤的人，只能告诉她"要看开，一切难过都会过去。"

让她知道她的身后有人支持着她，挺过这最难过的时刻。最重要是身体的康复，然后是心理的康复。

汕后悔以前和学生们交流得太少。可是这些想法也是遇到了事情才刚刚细细思量。汕想到要和 Loever 他们提议，学校应该请有关的专门老师增加青少年性健康讲座。

现实一点说，这么多年，汕个人的感情又得到什么，关于 K，仍然是音信全无。这已经不是什么关于爱情的小小游戏和玩笑了。

旖英喝了汕给她做的黄澄澄的鸡汤，泛出诱人的光

泽，旑英说："我似乎又恢复
过来了。"

"当然了，毕竟是年
轻人。"

11. 新生命

"其实，你的皮肤仍
然光泽美丽。"布兰儿双眼毫
不掩饰地赞美汕。"这是不
用化妆品的结果。"

汕自豪地告诉她。布
兰儿愈发举步维艰了。布兰儿
在晚饭后突然发烧，汕听见隔
壁传来隐隐的哭泣声。这哭泣
声使汕仿佛体会到婴儿在母体
内的躁动不安。

汕站在布兰儿的房间
里，不知所措，"陪我上医
院，"布兰儿带着哭腔无助地
说。

汕敢说，汕很害怕。因为布兰儿说她的临产期要过半个月，而汕害怕那个不安分的小生命要提前来到这个世界上。

"我要去叫车！"

"快去!"布兰儿几乎是绝望地喊着。

布兰儿进了产房，一个医生脸色白白地，强作镇静地跑出来:"病人的丈夫来了没有？"

汕的心一下子提到嗓子眼上。

"出了什么事？"

"产妇是大龄产妇，且有心脏病，处境很危险，手术需要签字。"医生说。

汕说："她的丈夫两天之内赶不回来，汕是她在此地的唯一朋友，汕可以签字吗？
"

医生："只能这样了
"

汕在手术单病人亲属
一栏上签上汕的名字"TT。
"

汕在医院走廊的长椅
上坐了下来，外面天暗了下来，
过了一会，雨声大作。布兰儿
的丈夫也许明天就到了，汕心
里暗忖。没有哪个时候如此刻
一样汕是如此地想念计西，想
起那一天黄昏，斜斜的雨肆意
着，汕着一件秋天的黄衣裳，
汕从周末空空的宿舍出来，心
里充满了失落，雨靴里灌满了
水，走起路来沉得抬不起脚，
这时一个湿漉漉的身影突然出
现在眼前，一点一点地抬头看，
那一双寒星在一瞬间电光火石，

什么都不用说了，那是汕们相
识的第二天。

湿漉漉的计西成了汕
生命中永远也写不完的省略号。
那一天旖英喝完汕给她做的鸡
汤。便问汕："老师，你一生
最想做的事情是什么？"

汕很想说："只爱一个男人
啊。"可是汕只是对旖英说：
"老师和别的人一样，没有什
么特别的理想。"

汕已经知道爱一个男人很重要，
爱过之后学会不爱也很重要。
没有必要让旖英知道这一点，
对她来说，爱是她目前唯一的
出路。

布兰儿早就把汕这一类人划到
不知是哪一类的人群里，而汕
的无着落并不阻止汕与布兰儿
的亲近，也许仅仅是布兰儿来
自大海，她的身上若隐若现地

有一点点计西身上的影子。在布兰儿患难的这一刻，只有汕一个人守在她的身边，这使汕不由得想起她的丈夫，汕总是不能想象出他的模样，他的样子确实与汕无关，但这个时候他是应该来的了。

12. 计西到来

计西汕看到一个高大的男人的身影朝这边移动，茶褐色的皮肤遮住了一切黑暗，他的脚步急急的，上身稍稍地向前倾斜，这使汕想起从前那个在站台上急急寻找着汕的计西，火车就要开动了，可他还是那么急急地，上身稍微倾斜地寻找着，这给汕一个十分孩子气的印象，汕甚至涌起一种母性的感觉：

男人脆弱时也像一个孩子。

汕没有任这种感情泛滥，少女的汕，以为自己就是那种心理坚强的女性，世界总会因为汕是女性而更温暖和柔和平静。汕没有让他亲吻汕的前额，他却一再把那条围巾一再帮汕系好:亲爱，你路上要小心，保重！汕着一身黑色衣服，提着沉重的行旅，站在乱七八糟的托运行旅旁，托运处的小伙子调侃地笑了笑，汕也一样笑了笑。

"TT,你不要在到处乱走了，好吗，要等我。"

"那你呢？你等汕吗？"

"我等你。"

多年前的对话声音犹在耳边。

"计西----------。"

汕几乎凄厉地叫着，医院里的长廊被这一声叫喊惊醒，很多神秘的一直紧闭的门突然露出一条条可疑的缝隙，

从门缝里夹着一张张地蓬头垢
面。

"计西,你来了！"汕
伤心地摇着他的胳膊，泪水决
了堤坝似的涌了出来。

"我不懂计西是谁。"
计西说。走廊的那头，一辆白
色的车缓缓地推了过来，汕看
见计西用那汕最熟悉不过的，
多次在汕记忆深处出现过的眼
睛急切地向那边张望。

计西弯下腰去，对着
布兰儿喃喃低语，布兰儿苍白
的脸被娇宠地，幸福得意，尽
管她刚刚从死亡线上回来，她
中年得子，幸福无边。

汕梦见许多许多的信
压在汕的身上，使汕感到窒息。

睡梦中，汕坠落到无
边无底的深渊中，许多熟悉的
面孔向汕涌来，这个境界⋯⋯

148

如果心无杂念，心无牵挂，则活在人世间也能领略到快乐和飘逸。汕心里知道，汕挣脱着，汕要在这人世间享乐，如果要轮回，也要再遇见计西，汕不要变成一颗草，正想着，计西德面孔出现，他的眼睛悲怅地看着随风而去的汕，情急中他仿佛力大无比，他伸出了手，抓住了汕的手……他救了汕。

汕醒来，旖英在汕的房间里吃饼干。

"老师，我回来了。"

"是吗？"汕心已经老。

13. 旖英返校了

旖英返校了。旖英的返校归功于她去年参加的画展，她的参展的那副《少女》救了他。那是一幅以她自己为模特的裸体油画习作，如果

149

Loever 知道这副画得奖，一定会那喃喃自语：世风日下，人心不古。艺术学院点名旖英可以免试专业直接升油画系，学校又招回旖英。

"老师，汕还要跟你学画画。"旖英说。

吃过晚饭，骑着自行车，一个人向城外驶去，每当有不顺心的事，只能走到郊外，把自己交给自然。

这个地方汕没有来过，不高的山脊上长着一些草，一群坟茔突兀地立在那里，不知名的玫瑰色的小花朵在坟茔旁灿然开放。

死者已矣。

他们一定不会感到孤独的了。但他们的生命可是曾经有爱。汕的心理渐渐蓄满了悲哀。生命是什么，是满怀希望地地来，还是带着不满意离去。人，对爱的渴求是永远没有限度的。

汕不知何故，如此多愁善感，仿佛一个凄婉的爱情故事向汕诉说着什么，这个故事远离都市，凄婉而温柔敦厚，那苍苍造化怀抱着这个故事。

汕知道她没有把生的意义全部解释清楚，但汕知道她已经把自己的爱给了自信和智慧兼具的计西。

一切都是注定的，有什么可以改变注定呢？

14.栀子花

汕走过一片树林夕阳的余晖仍然在燃烧着，倦鸟静静地栖息在各自的树上，林子的那边呢，透出一片白亮的云，象一座耀眼的山。

汕在山脚下摘到一朵打着骨朵的栀子花，汕把它插到案头的花瓶中。

一个人的阴影进入汕的感觉中。他站在门口，汕倏然回头，想象着他的眼睛深情地望着汕，想象着汕深情地叫他"计西"，可汕只是默默地看着他。

汕在心里想，这就是计西，虽然看不见他，可汕总能感觉得到他。

他看着汕桌子上的栀子花说："怎么，那些残花，你还没有去掉？"

他看着桌子上的《渴望生活》说："你怎么还在看这本书？"在这本书的扉页上有他送给汕的字迹："也许你会多次失败，最终你能表现你自己，而且那种表现会印证你的生活。"

"多年来，汕就只为这句话而活。"汕告诉了计西。

计西说："TT，你已经长大了。"

计西拨开汕的发丝，发现了汕额头上的沧桑。

"TT，"他低哑的声音雄浑激荡，他把他的嘴唇印上了汕的额头。

"TT，你真的值得汕爱。"他说。

"可以进来吗？"汕的背后响起了一个彬彬有礼的声音，打断了汕的沉思默想。

"当然可以。"

"TT，汕谢谢你照顾了布兰儿"

他拿着桌上的栀子花，说，这花真香。

他又指着《渴望生活》说，你也在《渴望生活》？

"你觉得惊讶？"汕问。

计西："汕以为只有汕一人喜欢这本书。'

"布兰儿不喜欢？"汕试探他。

"不，他是一个纯粹的家庭型女人，对艺术从不关心。"

汕说"那么看来汕是一个不太纯粹的女人了？"

"也许，你有点男人风范。"他不好意思起来。

"没关系，汕宁愿率真的丑陋，而不要虚伪的漂亮。"

"你真有意思。"他的眼睛突然充满生机的放亮，这一点汕再熟悉不过了。

"谢谢你最高的评介。"汕知道计西对女人的最高评介就是"很有意思。"他已经站起来准备告辞，他车转的身子愕然地停了一下，这时候暮色真的降临了。

人不能同时踏入一条河流，这是哲学家早就讲过的，过去的就过去了，就像日历本上撕下的无数张废纸一样，那些日子，总会或多或少在生命的年轮中划过一点点痕迹，或美丽或丑陋。

事实上，令汕吃惊的是，汕像女巫一样正在让时光倒流。这就是我与计西同时踏入若干年前我们曾一同踏入额那条河流。但这一次当然不同，我的感觉是我已经安排好的情节一步一步朝着原来的河流迈进。

旖英很久没有来我这儿了。这个学校除了布兰儿，觞，旖英，几乎没有别的朋友了。相信我对于他们，亦是一样的重要。如果哪一天他们都离开了我，不知去向，那么生活又会是怎么样的呢？这几日多看了佛书，总是喜欢想一想注定，缘分等等字眼。

15. Loever 住院

六月南方的天气很热，我刚到医院看望 Loever。Loever 今天早上突然晕倒住院了，血糖太低引起。

在学校公共汽车站牌下，旖英背着画夹，长发在脑后束成一把，一身宽松的白色

T恤，把一脸的黝黑映衬得泽泽有光。青春毕竟是青春，无论从哪个角度来欣赏，永远是美丽的。

"旖英，这么大的太阳还要去写生？"

"去植物园，那里是全市最阴凉的地方。"

旖英不再说话，公共汽车来了，旖英德黄头发一闪，就消失了。

只剩下汕一个人在站牌下发怔。汕真的羡慕旖英明显流露出来的轻松。她想不出旖英30岁的样子，除了轻松与美丽，还能有什么？一个女人拥有美丽与朝气，那算是相当成功的女人了。

昨天晚上，Loever还对汕谆谆教导："TT，我理解年轻人比较感情用事，谁没

有年轻过？我想以过来人的身
份提醒你一句，适可而止。"

汕知道坏事传千里，
但更让汕难过的是，Loever
一付我完全为你好的中肯态度，
弄得汕有口难辨。觞在一旁，
刻着他永远也刻不完的蜡纸。
那笔尖发出均匀的，无动于衷
的声音。

*今天读书笔记：读到
一句话："重生则轻利。"世
人都知道生命短暂，但既然重
生又无法轻利，所以世人无法
享受到太上老君炼丹的乐趣，
从这一点上说，现代人真的不
如古人智慧。*

16.又 闻到了栀子花
的香味

汕又闻到了栀子花的
香味。

"摘得太早了，骨朵还没有打开，未等到开放，它就会凋谢。"我告诉 Kay，情节与几年前的一模一样。悲哀的潮水慢慢地将我淹没。

"这可是夏天最后一朵栀子花，千辛万苦寻来的呢。"我说。

我的泪水无声地流了下来。天气真热，当我起身拿起一把湿毛巾，胡乱地搽干净脸上的泪滴。

"飘风不终朝，骤雨不终日，孰为此者？天地。天地尚不能久，何况人呼？"古典经书上这么说。

分离不可避免地，

但同时又是相聚的注定

159

永远在内心深处漂移

着

就像大海与陆地的分

离

就像春天与冬天

不能二者并存

然而有一天

你又会在街角的转角

再一次地出现

在我的梦里

在我的眼前……

1991.6．9

人间一世

天上一日

逝者如斯！

渴望很多很多的爱！

渴望被你拥抱，安全地闭上眼睛，等待你的亲吻

渴望在一个小小的角落施展很多被你激赏的爱情小阴谋

渴望痛快淋漓地流泪

洗涤心中烦闷

欸，似乎日子总也到不了头

想你……

——汕日记

Kay要离开了，汕把这篇日记夹在《渴望生活》书中，送给了Kay，

Kay的车子消失在小路的尽头……

161

Paper books have published in Chinese edition:

1. 最后的山歌/The Last Mountain Song (novel)
   ISBN:9789082592009

2. 一条失散多年的鱼 /A Long – Lost Fish
   ISBN:9789082592047

3. 困顿马语 /Whisperer of Exhausted Horse (poetry)
   ISBN:9789082592023

4. 橄榄园手写诗 /Crete Olive Tree Field (poetry)
   ISBN:9789082592030

5. 呼吸/The Breath
(poetry)
ISBN:9789082592016

6. 黄锦婷文集/The
Pavilion of Jin
(novel prose poetry)
ISBN:9789082592061

Paper books have

published in English&

Chinese edition:

7. 异域的舞蹈 1970s/
Faraway so Close
Dance 1970s (novel
poetry in English)

ISBN:9789082592054

Faraway so close
Dance 1970s (en&cn)

ISBN:978172
66-0699

8. 芭蕉树心 1993/
banana tree heart
1993 (English
edition)

ISBN:9789082592078

9. 乡愁与爱/
Nostalgia & Love
Poem

ISBN:9789082592085

10. 空心人
1991/Empty Heart
1991

ISBN:9789082592092

11. working poetry
9781790231522

The Author

空心人 1991/Empty Heart 1991 was originally created by the author Jinting Huang, was born in 1968, she has been working in a law school and now she lives in Holland, she enjoys writing and has published books of poetry, prose and novel, etc.

She likes to use "潛", "汕" or as the main name of character in her series of short story novels: Faraway so Close Dance 1970s; Empty Heart 1991; Banana Tree Heart 1993; 6 short stories from her collection Pavilion of Jin.

In some work she used the same name in another short story. The pronunciation of Shan in Chinese is the meaning of kindness. This writing habit is almost throughout all her works, forming her own uniqueness.
汕/shan: the fish swims. (fishing, swim)
潛/shan: tearfully
舢/shan: the boat

汕/shan: the fish swims. (fishing, swim)

www.ingramcontent.com/pod-product-compliance
Lightning Source LLC
Chambersburg PA
CBHW032015170626
46807CB00006B/2812